MELVIN

The Mischievous Mongoose

First Day of School

Wade Cameron

Illustrations By:
Joel Ray Pellerin

To order additional copies of this book, contact:
Xlibris LLC
1-888-795-4274
www.Xlibris.com
Orders@Xlibris.com

Dedication

I would like to dedicate this book to my Grandma
Brenetta Hunter.

It was a cool and breezy Monday morning all the neighborhood children were outside playing just in time as the sun started rising except for one mongoose who kept on snoozing.

Melvin the Mongoose was his given name but every day was not quite the same.

Melvin liked to explore the river and hills as every day was an adventure and thrill.

Melvin was told by Grandma Mongoose never to cross the dam line but he failed to listen as he went off on the countryside.

Melvin was so excited, because it was his first day of school as Grandma Mongoose hollered, "Wake up children! It's time for school."

She would remind them to have a great day, but first, she gave them an important lesson to say.

She would give them a hug and say, "Do your very best and remember to follow the golden rule and what better place to learn, than on your first day of school."

Melvin had an older brother his name was Kevin and when Melvin got in trouble guess who saved him he was three years older, which made him seven.

Grandma Mongoose would prepare porridge for the children, as Melvin would begin to lick his face because it was his favorite plate and he wanted the first taste.

Grandma Mongoose would carry their breakfast out of the hut as she said "Eat up children, there's plenty to eat," The children would get excited and begin stomping their feet.

After the children finished their breakfast, they would make their way to the gate as Grandma Mongoose shouted, "Kids wait! I have a special surprise for each of you to taste."

Grandma Mongoose would put a special surprise in both of their bags, as she warned them, "Put it away! Before it falls in the wrong hands."

Melvin and Kevin smiled at each other as Grandma waved goodbye. She would tell them, "Have a great day and enjoy the fries."

Melvin and Kevin were happy, because they had many things to learn, as Melvin imagined in his mind the teacher calling on him,

when it got to his turn. They made their way around the corner as they spotted their favorite mango tree they would climb the nearest branch, hoping to pick three.

Melvin and Kevin would pick and pick as many mangoes as they could as they complained, they were getting really full.

On their way to school, they would play games and share laughs, They would gaze over at one another to see who would say "on your mark!!!

They had loads of fun because they were the best of friends they liked to play games that made them pretend.

The first stop was always at Pulley the parrot's bird house, as every morning he would circle above the tree house, trying to find a small mouse.

Further down the hill lived Hubert the pig, as he stood under the fig tree eating piles of figs.

He would oink to let the others know he was coming, as he rolled in the mud just before bathing.

Just at the top of the trail lived Leonard the Chameleon when he got angry, his eyes would change colors.

Their favorite thing to do was take shortcuts through the fields, as they journeyed on through- picking fruits, climbing and swinging From trees.

Melvin and his friends would arrive at school in plenty of time, as they were the first students to stand in front of the line.

But first, Melvin and his friends waited for the school bell to ring, as he and his friends would check their bags to make sure they had their things.

Melvin's first class was spelling as Mrs. Green would ask the children to take out their books, and begin their writing.

Art class was next, and was Melvin's favorite part, as he waited patiently, for Mrs. Green to say start.

Mrs. Green was surprised as Melvin finished before the rest. Afterwards, she gave him an important job as a test. She asked him to be her special helper for the day, as he went around the classroom passing out clay.

Oh boy, Melvin was the best helper, doing all he could. Mrs. Green thanked him saying, "You're doing a great job, well done."

At story time, everyone gathered on the grass as Mrs. Green read a story from the past.

At Math, Melvin would use the counter to help him subtract and add, but he would have trouble, which made him very mad. After that it was lunch followed by recess, Melvin was a great classmate sharing with the rest.

Melvin was having a great day, but things were about to change. as, Melvin noticed trouble coming his way. From faraway, there were a group of hens, coming closer and closer, Melvin counted ten.

The hens were causing trouble and running through the crowds, As they started chasing everyone, buuck buuck buuukcuck!!!! really loud.

Melvin went over to see if everything was alright, but the hens teased him and weren't being very nice. The hens circle him, and started to peck his tail, as Melvin said, "Hey! You guys are not playing fair!"

That's when Melvin started to chase the hens all around the playground, as his friends joined in, and everyone started making all kinds of sounds.

Mrs. Green rushed over, to break up the fight, as she pointed, "Go to the principal's office!" as she wasn't going to repeat it twice.

Mr. Bull was sitting in his office, as Melvin knocked on the door. He replied, "Come in, and sit on the floor."

Melvin explained the entire story, from beginning to end, as Melvin told Mr. Bull the hens teased me, and didn't want to be my friend.

That's when Mr. Bull told them an important life lesson, that in order to make friends, they had to play nice.

For the rest of the week, Mr. Bull gave Melvin and Kevin an important job after school, as they wrote on the board, 'I will follow the golden rule.'

From that day on, Melvin the Mischievous Mongoose was his given name, because when trouble was near-guess who was to blame? But he learned an important lesson, each and every day.

The End

CPSIA information can be obtained
at www.ICGtesting.com
Printed in the USA
LVIC04n2307050814
397701LV00005B/12

*9 7 8 1 4 7 9 7 0 2 7 0 1 *